MS. FROGBOTTOM'S FIELD TRIPS

★ FANGS FOR HAVING US! ★

By **SOFIA**, *as told to* **NANCY KRULIK**
Illustrated by **HARRY BRIGGS**

ALADDIN

New York London Toronto Sydney New Delhi

ALADDIN
An imprint of Simon & Schuster Children's Publishing Division
1230 Avenue of the Americas, New York, New York 10020
First Aladdin hardcover edition July 2021
Text copyright © 2021 by Nancy Krulik
Illustrations copyright © 2021 by Harry Briggs
Also available in an Aladdin paperback edition.
For information about special discounts for bulk purchases, please contact
Simon & Schuster Special Sales at 1-866-506-1949 or business@simonandschuster.com.
The Simon & Schuster Speakers Bureau can bring authors to your live event.
For more information or to book an event contact the Simon & Schuster Speakers
Bureau at 1-866-248-3049 or visit our website at www.simonspeakers.com.
Jacket designed by Karin Paprocki
Interior designed by Mike Rosamilia
The illustrations for this book were rendered digitally.
The text of this book was set in Neutraface Slab Text.
Manufactured in the United States of America 0621 FFG
2 4 6 8 10 9 7 5 3 1
Library of Congress Control Number 2020952957
ISBN 9781534454033 (hc)
ISBN 9781534454026 (pbk)
ISBN 9781534454040 (ebook)

For Ian, who really knows how
to take a bite out of life
—N. K.

WELCOME TO CLASS 4A.

We have a warning for you:

BEWARE OF THE MAP.

Our classroom probably looks a lot like yours. We have chairs, desks, a whiteboard, and artwork on the walls. And of course we have our teacher, Ms. Frogbottom.

Actually, our teacher is the reason why things sometimes get strange around here. Because Ms. Frogbottom is kind of *different*.

For starters, she carries around a backpack. It looks like any other pack, but somehow strange things always seem to be popping out of it. You don't have to worry about most of the stuff our teacher carries. But if she reaches into her pack and pulls out her giant map, beware. That map is *magic*. It has the power to lift us right out of our classroom and drop us in some faraway place. And somehow it's always the exact same time as when we left. No matter where we go, we wind up meeting frightening creatures none of us ever believed were real—and getting into all sorts of trouble.

You don't have to be *too* scared, though. Things always seem to turn out okay for us in the end. Or at least they have *so far*....

Your new pals,

Aiden, Emma, Oliver, Olivia, Sofia, and Tony

MS. FROGBOTTOM'S FiELD TRiP DO'S anD DON'TS

- Do stay together.

- Don't take photos. You can't experience the big world through a tiny camera hole.

- Don't bring home souvenirs. We want to leave the places we visit exactly as we found them.

- Don't use the word "weird." The people, places, and food we experience are just different from what you are used to.

- Do have fun!

1

"WHO WANTS TO HEAR A SPOOKY STORY?"
Olivia asks as she finishes the last bite of her hot dog. "I know a great one."

"Not me," Tony tells her. "I don't like being scared." He grows quiet for minute and listens to something. "Did you hear footsteps in the woods? I think it was a bear. Have I mentioned that I'm scared of bears?"

"It's just the wood crackling in the campfire," Olivia's twin brother, Oliver, assures him. "You're imagining things."

"I wonder why marshmallows taste so much better when they're cooked over a fire," Aiden says.

"Because the extreme heat makes the sugar caramelize," I explain. "That changes the flavor of the marshmallow so it's more buttery."

Aiden rolls his eyes. "I wasn't really asking."

Well, how was I supposed to know that? He said "I wonder." That usually means someone wants an answer.

"Is there anything you *don't* know, Sofia?" Emma asks me. She fixes the daisy crown on her head and pops a marshmallow into her mouth.

I don't answer Emma. I know *she's* not really asking. She's just finding another way to call me the class brain. Our teacher, Ms. Frogbottom, has made it clear she doesn't like name-calling. And "class brain" is definitely name-calling.

It's not like I can help having the kind of memory that lets me remember everything I read or see. It's just the way my mind works.

Sometimes having a great memory can be really helpful. Like today, when our class got lost hiking around science camp. Ms. Frogbottom had left her map of the campground back in her tent. But she'd shown us the map earlier, so I'd memorized all the hiking trails. When we got lost on our hike, I was the one who got us back to our campsite.

I love being at science camp. Our class is here for two whole days, studying nature and sleeping under the stars. Today we did experiments to find out what kinds of minerals are in the soil. Tomorrow we're going to test the creek water for bacteria. This is my kind of field trip!

We aren't the only kids at the campground. Right now there are other classes sprinkled around the woods, sitting at their own fires, eating marshmallows and telling ghost stories. For them this is probably their biggest adventure for the whole school year.

But not for our class. We go on *a lot* of

field trips. Ms. Frogbottom says people learn best from experiencing things. So she takes us out of school really often. Which we all love.

Well, *almost* all of us love it, anyway. Tony's not too sure.

"Do you think there really are bears in the woods?" he asks nervously.

Ms. Frogbottom smiles from across the campfire she built near our class's campsite. "There may be," she says calmly. "But as long as we clean up our trash and don't leave any food around, the bears should leave us alone."

Tony starts biting nervously at the skin around his nails—which is kind of gross, since he still has dirt under his fingernails from this morning's experiments. "I hate field trips," he complains. "They're always so scary."

"Come on, Tony," Oliver replies. "Bears would be the least scary creatures we've met up with on one of Ms. Frogbottom's field trips."

I know what Oliver means. Ms. Frogbottom has taken us on some pretty *interesting* trips.

Once, she took us to Egypt, where we saw the pyramids and the tombs of the great pharaohs. That part was really fun. But meeting a living mummy who wanted to hold us prisoner in his tomb of doom sure wasn't.

Another time Ms. Frogbottom took

us to Scotland. While we were there, we came face-to-face with the Loch Ness Monster! He was HUGE. To make things worse, Tony nearly drowned.

You may be wondering how our class can travel all over the world on field trips and still get back in time for dismissal. No airplane goes *that* quickly.

But we don't travel by plane.

Or train.

Or even bus.

We actually travel by map. Or more specifically, Ms. Frogbottom's *Magic Map*. The huge one she carries in her backpack.

Ordinarily I don't believe in magic. I've always thought there was a scientific explanation for anything that happens in the universe. But I can't think of any explanation for how Ms. Frogbottom's map works, unless it's by magic. Because when Ms. Frogbottom points her finger at a place anywhere in the world, we are suddenly taken there—in a matter of seconds.

So you can imagine how curiously we are all staring at our teacher now, as she reaches into her backpack. Is she about to pull out the Magic Map? Are we about to be magically transported from science camp to someplace far away?

Nope. Ms. Frogbottom was just reaching for a red plastic back scratcher. She's using it to scratch at the mosquito bites on her back.

"Aaaah," our teacher says. "That's better."

"The mosquitoes at science camp are vicious," Emma says. She scratches at her arm. "I think one of them bit me three times."

"Impossible," Aiden tells her. "After a mosquito bites you, it dies."

"That's not true," I tell Aiden. "Female mosquitoes bite people to get their blood. Then they use that blood to nourish their eggs. In its six-week lifetime, a mosquito lays eggs over and over again—up to two hundred eggs at a time! Which means mosquitoes have to bite a lot of people. Some more than once."

Emma smiles proudly. "See?" she tells Aiden.

★ 14 ★

Aiden frowns and mumbles something under his breath. It sounds a lot like "class brain."

"I don't have mosquito bites." Tony fingers the small cloth bag that's hanging from a leather rope around his neck. "My nonna's garlic keeps mosquitoes away."

"It also keeps your *friends* away." Oliver laughs. "You stink."

Tony shrugs. "Maybe. But I'm the only one of us who's not scratching."

I know it's probably not Tony's grandmother's garlic that's keeping the mosquitoes away. More likely it's something in the chemical makeup of Tony's sweat that's stopping them from biting him.

For a minute I think about calling

up an article on my tablet so Tony can read about that. Then I remember that I'm not getting service in the woods. My tablet is pretty much worthless here, which is driving me nuts. I hate when I can't immediately get the information I want.

"So about my scary story . . . ," Olivia reminds us all.

"No, no, no!" Tony exclaims.

"You can listen or not, Tony," Olivia insists. "But I'm telling it. Once upon a time there was a camper who snuck out of his tent and wandered off—"

Swish!

"AAAAAH!" Before Olivia can go any further, Tony screams.

 ★ 16 ★

"I didn't even get to the scary part yet," Olivia tells him.

"Something just *swished* right over my head!" Tony answers.

"Probably a bat," I tell him. "I bet there are a lot of them here. With all the mosquitoes, they have plenty to eat."

My friends stare at me.

"What?" I wonder. "You guys know bats eat mosquitoes."

"Sure," Oliver agrees. "But why didn't *you* know it was a bad idea to tell Tony that there are plenty of bats *here*?"

"Bats are horrible," Tony says nervously. "They'll bite you and suck the blood right out of your neck."

"There are such things as vampire bats," I agree. "And they do feed on blood."

Tony keeps nervously chewing the skin around his fingernails.

"Sofia, stop," Oliver pleads. "Look what you're doing to him."

"Vampire bats don't bite people," I assure Tony. "Only animals. Usually cows."

Tony looks at me. "Are you sure?"

I nod. "Absolutely."

Tony glances across the campfire to Ms. Frogbottom. "Is Sofia right?"

Ms. Frogbottom nods. "Bats are not the enemy, Tony. They eat the bugs that annoy us. I've always been fascinated by them. Now that you've brought them up . . ." Ms. Frogbottom reaches into her backpack and pulls out her Magic Map.

If Tony was scared before, he looks absolutely petrified now. "*I* didn't bring them up," he insists. "That bat brought itself up. It flew right over my head."

But our teacher isn't listening. She's busy looking for a place on her map. A giant smile forms on her face. She taps the map with her finger.

Suddenly a white light flashes all around us. My body feels weightless, and I think my feet have just left the ground.

It's like I'm flying in space. And then . . .

2

"WHOA!" OLIVER EXCLAIMS. "THIS IS *NOT* science camp."

"Where are we?" Olivia asks.

Ms. Frogbottom smiles. "Where do you *think* we are? Put the facts together. I'll bet you can figure it out."

I look down at the cobblestones beneath my feet. Then I look up at the full moon. By the moonlight I can see that the concrete houses lining the road are close together and mostly painted in pale colors—pink, yellow, blue, and green. The windows have wood trim.

The roads are narrow and winding, leading up and down steep hills. The cars parked on the street are much smaller than the ones we have at home. The license plates on the cars look different too—they're longer and thinner, and there's an *RO* in the corner of each one.

I wish I could hear people talking. Maybe I would recognize the language. But it's dinnertime and everyone is inside, eating. The small street is empty.

"Those homes seem hundreds of years old," I say. "We could be somewhere in Europe. The houses in Europe are often older than the ones at home."

"Very good," Ms. Frogbottom says. "But *where* in Europe?"

"This all started when we were sitting around the fire," Emma thinks out loud. "Maybe we're someplace that burned down once."

I shake my head. "Can't be. The old houses wouldn't still be here if there had been a big fire."

I hear Emma mutter "class brain" under her breath. It's hard for me not to feel bad.

"Wait," Olivia says. "Weren't we talking about bats? Maybe we're in some place where you would find a lot of bats."

"I don't think this is Yankee Stadium," Oliver jokes.

"Olivia's right," I say. "I think we *are* in a place known for its bats. The flying ones—not the baseball kind." I turn to Ms. Frogbottom. "*RO* could stand for 'Romania.' Are we in Transylvania, Romania?"

"Yes!" Ms. Frogbottom cheers. "You figured it out. We are in the Sighişoara area of Transylvania, Romania."

"I've heard of Transylvania," Emma

says. "It's where Dracula came from. I saw the movie. In it Dracula was—"

"A vampire." The words are out of my mouth before I can stop them. I shouldn't have said that. I know vampires aren't real.

I also know that just the thought of vampires will scare Tony. But I've already said it. And sure enough . . .

"VAMPIRE?" Tony shouts.

"There was no Dracula," I assure Tony. "He was just a made-up character in a book."

"You mean a movie," Emma says.

"It was a book first," I tell her. "A *fiction* book."

But that doesn't make Tony happier.

"I want to go back to science camp," he moans.

"There are mosquitoes here," Aiden says as he scratches at a fresh bug bite. "Just like at science camp."

"You didn't like camp," Oliver reminds Tony. "You were afraid of the bears."

"Bears aren't as scary as vampires," Tony insists.

I turn on my tablet. *Phew*. I'm getting a signal here.

"Actually, Transylvania has one of the largest bear populations in all of Europe," I say as I scroll through an article I just found. "And of course, where there are mosquitoes, there are usually bats. Which is why I think people tell vampire stories around here."

"Bears, bats, *and* vampires?" Tony sounds terrified.

"Wait a minute," Emma says. "This can't be Transylvania. If it were, Dracula's castle would be up on top of a giant hill."

"You're talking about Bran Castle," I tell Emma. "The model for the castle in the book *Dracula*." I scroll a little further on my tablet. "That's in Bran, which is another part of Transylvania. "

"Good," Tony says. "Because I don't want to be anywhere near anything that had to do with Dracula."

"There was no Dracula," I repeat, looking at my tablet. "Oh, this is interesting. . . ."

"What is?" Olivia asks me.

"I don't want to know," Tony groans.

"It says that the author of the book *Dracula*, Bram Stoker, based the made-up character of Count Dracula on a real Romanian prince named Vlad the Impaler. Vlad wasn't a vampire, but he *was* a really mean guy."

"Okay, then I don't want to meet *Vlad*," Tony says.

FROGBOTTOM FACTS

★ Bram Stoker published his book *Dracula* in 1897.
★ Bram Stoker got the name "Dracula" from Vlad the Impaler's family name, "Dracul," which is Latin for Dracula.

"You won't meet him," I promise Tony. "He died in 1476."

"I want to go back to science camp," Tony whimpers.

"Nonsense," Ms. Frogbottom tells him. "We just got here. There's so much to see."

"We can't see *anything*," Tony insists. "It's dark out. And that's when vampires appear. Right?"

I shake my head. "There are no such things as vampires."

"I've seen *a lot* of vampire movies," Emma insists, like that makes her some kind of expert on the subject. "Vampires have difficulty seeing in the daytime, so they come out at night. And they're shape-shifters—"

"Like the kelpie we met in Scotland?" Aiden pipes up. "He turned from a man into a horse."

"Kind of," Emma replies. "But in vampire movies they change from people into bats. That lets them fly off quickly when they're in trouble."

"I'd love to be able to fly off anytime I got in trouble," Olivia says.

"You'd be flying an awful lot," Oliver tells his sister. "You might never land."

"What else do you know about vampires?" Aiden asks Emma.

"Vampires aren't re—" I begin.

But Emma interrupts me. She loves showing off all her vampire knowledge. Except it isn't really knowledge, because these aren't facts. They're just made-up legends she's seen play out in the movies.

"Vampires can be scared off with garlic, a group of them is called a brood, and they don't have any reflections, so they can't see themselves in a mirror," Emma tells our classmates.

"You'd better never become a vampire," Aiden tells Emma. "You'd go nuts if you couldn't look in the mirror."

Emma sticks her tongue out at Aiden. But she doesn't argue. Instead she keeps talking about vampires in the movies. She's acting like such a know-it-all. A *vampire* know-it-all.

And now no one wants to hear any of the *real* facts I've found on my tablet.

Which is a shame, because they're really interesting.

Vlad the Impaler was held hostage for six years by the Ottomans when he was a boy. When he grew up and became a leader, he ordered the killing of more than twenty thousand Ottomans as revenge. Just for fun he would invite his enemies to dinner, and then kill them.

That's real information. But all anyone wants to hear about is the made-up stuff Emma's seen in the movies.

"Vampires hypnotize their victims to make it easier to lure them into the vampires' lairs and bite their necks," Emma continues. "Once a person is bitten by a vampire, they become one too."

★ 33 ★

Tony puts his hands over his ears. "Stop!" he cries. "I don't want to hear anything else about Dracula *or* the Vlad guy."

"Well, actually," Ms. Frogbottom says, "Vlad the Impaler was born right around here, in 1431."

Tony's eyes grow huge. "He-e-re?" he says with a gulp.

"In that house." Ms. Frogbottom points to a very normal-looking pale yellowish-tan concrete home. There are small windows in different places on the front of the house, with a pretty flower box beneath each window.

It's hard to believe that a guy nicknamed Vlad the Impaler could have been born in such a peaceful-looking house.

"Impaling" means sticking a spear or a stake through someone's body. It makes the victim die really slowly and with a lot of pain. That's not peaceful.

"Can we go inside?" Aiden asks.

"Well, they *have* turned the house into a restaurant and museum," Ms. Frogbottom begins. "But it's closed at night. So—"

"URA! URA!"

Ms. Frogbottom is drowned out by screams coming from just around the bend. It sounds like there's a whole crowd of people storming through the streets.

The shouts are in a different language, so I don't know what the people are saying. All I can tell is that there are a lot of them! *And they're coming our way.*

"Wow!" Olivia exclaims as a huge crowd turns the corner and stomps toward us.

"What's that guy in the front of the line carrying?" Tony cries. "It looks like a giant spear. They're going to stab us all!"

"You mean *impale* us all!" I correct him. But no one hears me over the cries of the oncoming mob.

"Ura! Ura!"

3

THE CROWD IS GETTING CLOSER AND
closer.

The shouts are getting louder and
louder.

And the spear . . .

Wait a minute. I don't think that's a
spear after all. For one thing, the long pole
doesn't have a point on it. You'd need a
point if you were going to impale someone. And for another thing, it's covered in

brightly colored handkerchiefs and little bells. Most warriors wouldn't take time to decorate their spears.

"Oh my! It's an evening wedding parade!" Ms. Frogbottom cheers. "You see how the best man is holding the wedding pole? He did a wonderful job decorating it. It's such a happy symbol of a strong marriage."

I *knew* that stick wasn't a spear.

People are coming out of their houses to watch the parade. There's a lot of cheering in the streets now.

"URA! URA!"

I guess those weren't battle cries. They were cheers for the bride and groom.

"Where's the bride?" Emma asks.

"She's the one with the crown that's

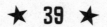

covered in flowers, jewels, and ribbons," Ms. Frogbottom replies. "The groom is the man in the felt hat that's decorated with feathers and flowers. You see him there? He's wearing the white leather vest."

"Are their clothes traditional Romanian folk costumes?" I ask Ms. Frogbottom, pointing to the brightly embroidered skirts and puffy white blouses worn by the women in the parade.

"Yes," Ms. Frogbottom tells me.

"So Romanian brides don't get to wear long white gowns?" Emma asks. She sounds disappointed.

"Some do," Ms. Frogbottom assures her. "But others dress in the same costumes their ancestors wore hundreds of years ago."

Our teacher reaches into her backpack and pulls out a huge handful of uncooked rice, which she tosses at the bride and groom. "Wishing you good fortune!" she shouts as she throws.

We watch as the parade passes by, with the people singing and laughing. Now that they're closer, I can tell they're happy. I can't believe we were ever afraid of them.

As the wedding party travels on, the other villagers return to their homes. A cloud passes across the full moon, and everything gets a bit darker and gloomier.

AROOOOOOOO! As if things weren't eerie enough, now an animal is howling at the moon.

And then an awful smell fills the air.

"What's that?" Aiden asks. He holds his nose.

"It stinks," Olivia adds. "Worse than that garlic around Tony's neck."

"I told you we should get out of here," Tony says. He turns slightly and looks over his shoulder. "Oh no. We *can't* get out of here!"

"Why not?" Olivia asks him.

"There's a wall surrounding us." Tony points toward the circle of ancient stone walls and towers surrounding the city. "I bet it was built to hold people prisoner!"

"I don't think those walls were built to hold people in," I tell Tony. "More likely they were built to keep enemies *out*. I'm

FROGBOTTOM FACTS

★ The protective citadel walls around Sighişoara were built way back in the 1100s.
★ The Clock Tower, which is also called the gate tower, marked the main entrance to the city.
★ At almost 210 feet, the Clock Tower is tall enough to be seen from anywhere in Sighişoara.

sure there are gates. We can just walk through one of them."

"What if the gates are locked?" Tony asks.

"It won't matter. We've got an easier way out." Oliver points to Ms. Frogbottom, who is already pulling the Magic Map from her backpack.

"Here we go again," Emma says.

"I wonder where to," Olivia says.

We're about to find out. Ms. Frogbottom

★ 43 ★

has placed her finger on the map.

Suddenly a white light flashes all around us. My body feels weightless, and I think my feet have just left the ground.

It's like I'm flying in space. And then . . .

"THIS STREET LOOKS KIND OF LIKE THE last one, but it's not exactly the same," Olivia says as we study our new surroundings.

"That's because we're in a different part of Transylvania," I tell her. "This area is called Bran."

"How do you know?" Oliver asks.

"Because that's *Bran* Castle," I say, pointing over his shoulder at a fortress

that's terra-cotta-orange and white, with pointed towers and tiny windows. It sits high atop a mountain overlooking the village. The castle is shrouded by trees, and the way the branches are blowing under the moonlight makes the castle seem extra creepy.

"*Dracula's* Castle!" Emma exclaims. "It looks just like it does in the movies."

"Count Dracula was fake," I insist.

"Well, the castle is *real*," Emma tells me.

Just then a bat flies out from one of the castle windows. It flaps its wings beneath the moon.

Grumble.

"What was that?" Tony jumps three feet into the air.

Aiden laughs. "My stomach. I'm hungry."

"You ate five hot dogs at science camp," Oliver says.

FROGBOTTOM FACTS

★ Bran Castle was named for its location, the village of Bran, which is in the Transylvania area of Romania.

★ The construction of Bran Castle began in 1377. It was finished eleven years later, in 1388.

★ Bran Castle was originally used as a fortress, and soldiers lived there. The castle later became home to Queen Marie of Romania and the royal family.

"So what?" Aiden asks. "Ms. Frogbottom, do you think there's a place around here where we can get something to eat?"

"In most European cities there's a café in the town square," our teacher tells him. "I just have to figure out where the square is."

"I think it must be that way," I say, pointing left.

"Why would you say that?" Ms. Frogbottom wonders.

"That's where those people are coming from." I point to a group of adults who are laughing as they walk toward us. "The bald man has a fresh grease stain on his shirt. And the woman in the long skirt is carrying what looks like a box of leftover food. They must be coming from a restaurant."

"Excellent deductive reasoning, Sofia!" Ms. Frogbottom cheers.

Aiden gives me a grateful look. I bet now he's happy that I'm such a brain.

A few minutes later we're seated at an outdoor café. All around us people are eating hungrily. I don't blame them. The food smells delicious.

A waiter walks over to our table. "What can I get you?" he asks.

"We'd like to try traditional Romanian food," Ms. Frogbottom tells him. "But not too much. We're really only here for a bite."

Tony gulps. "Did she say *a bite*?"

"This café is so pretty," Emma says. "It looks just like the outdoor restaurants you see in old movies."

"Old *vampire* movies?" Olivia wonders.

Emma nods. "There was this movie I saw where the vampire turned into a bat and hung upside down in a tree, watching his next victim eat dinner."

"Trees like those?" Aiden asks, pointing to three large trees not far from our table.

"Exactly," Emma says. "I wonder if there are vampire bats in those branches."

I doubt it. Because, like I told everyone before, vampire bats feed on cows' blood. There are no cows around here.

But there *is* something very strange going on near those trees. A skinny man with thick, dark eyebrows is watering the flowers at the base of the tree trunks.

"That's odd," I say.

"What is?" Emma asks me.

"That man is gardening," I tell her.

"So what?" Emma replies.

"The sun's gone down," I explain. "Have you ever heard of anyone gardening by moonlight?"

Emma shrugs and goes back to talking about vampire movies. But I'm not listening to her. I'm too busy looking at the gardener.

The fact that he's working in the dark isn't the strangest thing about this man.

When he thinks no one is looking, he captures a mosquito in his hands. And he *eats* it. Just like a bat.

I look to see if any of my classmates saw that too.

Apparently not. They were all too busy listening to Emma.

RUFF, RUFF, ROOOOO!

"Did you hear that?" Aiden asks. "They sure have loud dogs in Romania."

"It doesn't sound like any dog I've ever heard," I tell him. "It could be a wolf."

"Maybe it's a *werewolf*," Tony suggests.

"It's not a werewolf," the mosquito-eating gardener says, walking over to our table.

"That's good." Tony sounds relieved.

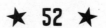

"More likely it's a capcaun," the gardener continues matter-of-factly. "They're related to dogs."

"Like foxes?" Aiden wonders.

"Not exactly," the man continues. "Capcauns are ogres with dog faces.

They have four eyes. And . . ." A creepy smile comes over his face. "Their favorite food is human meat. Especially meat from *young* humans. Capcauns trick children into entering the forest. Then they eat them. Luckily, capcauns have a terrible odor. It acts as a warning. If you smell something in the forest that turns your stomach, stay away."

The gardener nods at Ms. Frogbottom. "I am sorry to have interrupted," he apologizes.

"Not at all," our teacher replies. "I'm sure my class found that fascinating, Mr. . . ."

"Sange," the gardener says.

"I'm Ms. Frogbottom."

"We smelled something really awful

after that wedding parade," Olivia recalls.

"And we heard howling," Emma adds. "It could have been a capcaun."

"I doubt it," I tell her. "A four-eyed dog-ogre isn't exactly something you'd see in the natural world."

"But it is something you'd see in the *supernatural* world," Emma argues.

"I wouldn't worry about running into some character from a folktale," I say.

"Yeah," Aiden agrees. "Especially since right now all I smell is *food*. Here comes our waiter with the grub."

"Grubs are delicious," Mr. Sange remarks.

Aiden laughs. I'm not so sure Mr. Sange is kidding.

"Lamb *drob* is our specialty." The waiter

places a slice of meat loaf onto each of our plates.

"The *drob* here is wonderful," Mr. Sange tells us. "There's a surprise in every piece."

"I don't need any more surprises," Tony complains.

"Relax," Oliver says. "I think the surprise is the hard-boiled egg in the middle of the meat."

"Indeed." Mr. Sange turns to Ms. Frogbottom. "Perhaps after your meal I can

FROGBOTTOM FaCT

★ Traditional Romanian recipes are based on foods eaten by the people who invaded the country during the Middle Ages. Romanian food is often influenced by Turkish, Hungarian, German, and Austrian recipes.

arrange a private tour of Bran Castle for you. I'm the groundskeeper there, and I have my own key. You can't come to Transylvania without visiting Bran Castle."

"Sure we can," Tony mutters.

If Ms. Frogbottom heard Tony, she's ignoring him, because she exclaims, "That would be wonderful!"

"Excellent," Mr. Sange says. "But first you eat." He pulls up a chair and sits beside Ms. Frogbottom. In the moonlight I can see that he has unusual eyes: one blue and one green.

"Do you have ketchup?" Oliver asks the waiter.

"I'm sorry," the waiter replies. "We don't serve ketchup."

"I've got some." Ms. Frogbottom reaches into her backpack and pulls out ketchup. I don't mean a few of those little packets that you might get at a fast-food restaurant. For some reason Ms. Frogbottom has been lugging around a giant bottle of ketchup in her backpack. "Here you go."

"You pour ketchup onto everything," Olivia says to her brother. "You'd put it on your cereal if Mom would let you."

"I like ketchup," Oliver says with a shrug. "It makes my food taste better."

"This tastes pretty good on its own," Tony says. "But not as good as my nonna's meat loaf. She puts a lot of garlic in hers."

"The chef at this café does not cook with garlic," Mr. Sange admits. "But there are plenty of delicious spices in the food, like basil, rosemary, and tarragon."

"You don't need any more garlic," Emma tells Tony. "Your neck already smells. You want your breath to stink too?"

"Emma!" Ms. Frogbottom scolds.

"I'm sorry," Emma apologizes to Tony. "But your necklace really smells awful."

"It's working, though," Tony says. "Still no mosquito bites."

"What's wrong with a little bite of mosquito?" Mr. Sange asks.

We all stare at him, but no one says a word.

How do you answer a question like that?

"I WONDER HOW THEY WERE ABLE TO build a castle on the top of this mountain more than six hundred years ago," Olivia says as we hike toward Bran Castle. "They didn't have trucks back then."

"The mountain is really steep," Emma agrees. "Good thing I'm wearing my new hiking boots. They're very comfortable and . . ."

OWOOOOOO!

Whatever Emma is saying is drowned out by a howling coming from the surrounding forest.

"Do you think that's a capcaun?" Tony asks nervously.

"No," I reply.

"That castle looks like something straight out of a scary movie," Aiden remarks.

He's not wrong. With its pointy towers shooting up toward the cloud-covered full moon, Bran Castle really does look frightening. I can see why Bram Stoker chose to use it as the model for Dracula's castle in his book.

Even the walk up to the castle is nerve-wracking. It's dark out, and there isn't another soul on the road—probably because there's nothing at the top but the castle, and it's closed to tourists tonight. There are thick forests on either side of us. Every now and then you can hear an animal stepping on a dried twig, or a bat squeaking in the night, or—

OWOOOOOO!

"There it goes again," Tony says. "Whatever's out there is giving us a warning."

"What kind of warning?" Oliver wonders.

"To stay out of the castle," Tony replies.

"If that's true, we'd probably be better off *inside* Bran Castle," Oliver insists.

Tony gives Oliver a funny look. "How do you figure that?"

"Remember what Mr. Sange said about capcauns tricking kids?" Oliver reminds him. "What if it *is* a capcaun that's howling? What if it's trying to *fool* us into staying out here?"

"Oliver has a point," I tell Tony. "Places like Bran Castle were built to protect people from their enemies. If capcauns actually existed, they would definitely be our enemy. So logically we'd be safer inside the castle than out. But honestly, Tony, there's nothing to be scared of. There are no such things as capcauns—or vampires." I add that last part for Emma.

"Come along," Ms. Frogbottom urges. "We just have to climb up these stairs, and then we'll be at the doors of Bran Castle."

Just have to climb up these stairs? Ms. Frogbottom makes that seem like no big deal. But there are hundreds of steps. They're hard and rocky, which makes the climbing even more difficult.

Still, I'm not stopping. I want to know what's inside Bran Castle.

FROGBOTTOM FACT

★ You have to climb almost fifteen hundred steps to reach the base of Bran Castle.

6

"WE DID IT! WE REACHED THE CASTLE!"
Aiden pumps his fist in the air and cheers
when we arrive at the arched doorway of
Bran Castle.

"Welcome," Mr. Sange says as he opens
the door.

We follow him into a small entryway.
The room is dark, with wooden walls that
are decorated with old portraits of men in
rich velvet capes, and a huge mirror with

a fancy gold frame. The only light is coming from a few candles and the full moon outside.

"This is exactly the way I imagined a vampire's castle," Emma says as she fixes her hair in the old dusty mirror.

"Me too," Tony murmurs. "Spooky."

"I think they make it look this way for tourists," I assure him.

"Velcome to Bran Castle." I turn to see a tall man with dark, slicked-back hair standing behind us. He's really pale—his face looks almost as white as the shirt under his red-and-black cape.

FROGBOTTOM FACT

★ Nearly 800,000 tourists visit Bran Castle each year.

"Master," Mr. Sange says. "I have brought you fresh blood."

Master? What a strange thing to call someone, even if you work for him.

Tony's eyes open wide. "Fresh *blood*?"

"I meant new guests," Mr. Sange corrects himself. "My English isn't always so good."

"I vant you to make yourselves at home," the man in the red-and-black cape says with a thick accent. "The night is young. Our fun has just begun. I'm Mr. Liliac, and I vill be your host for the evening."

Ms. Frogbottom smiles at him. "Pleased to meet you," she says. "I'm Ms. Frogbottom. Thank you for allowing us to visit the castle after hours. It's an honor to be the only guests in such a famous place."

"I'm sure you vill enjoy yourselves," Mr. Liliac replies. "Most of my guests vant to stay *forever*."

Mr. Sange lets out a strange, cackling laugh.

Mr. Liliac turns to the groundskeeper. "Thank you for bringing me new victims," he says.

"I think you mean '*visitors*,'" Ms. Frogbottom corrects him.

"Yes." Mr. Liliac smiles at Ms. Frogbottom. "Of course."

"It is my pleasure to serve you, master," Mr. Sange tells Mr. Liliac. "But I must be on my way. The castle gardens won't tend themselves."

"Feel free to look around the room,"

Mr. Liliac tells us as Mr. Sange leaves. "My home is your home."

A while later Emma pulls me aside. "There's something strange about Mr. Liliac," she whispers. "I think he's a real vampire."

"He's an actor, pretending to be mysterious," I insist. "That way tourists feel like they're having a real Transylvanian experience."

Emma shakes her head. "He's not acting."

I roll my eyes. "Come on, Emma. Taking a few acting classes doesn't make you an expert."

"It's not that. Remember what I said about vampires not having any reflections? Mr. Liliac was standing right behind me when I was looking in the mirror. But I didn't see him. It was like he wasn't there. *Except he was.*"

I'm not sure what to say. Emma sometimes exaggerates things.

"And did you notice that Mr. Liliac is staying as far from Tony as possible?" Emma continues. "He pointed out that sword to Aiden, Oliver, and Olivia. And he told you and me about Queen Marie's heart being buried near here. But Mr. Liliac hasn't said a single word to Tony. I think he doesn't want to get too close to that pouch of garlic."

"None of that proves anything," I insist. "Because there's nothing to prove. There are no such things as vampires."

Emma glares at me.

"Was Vlad close to his brother?" I hear Olivia asking Mr. Liliac.

"There vas a great deal of *bad blood* between them," Mr. Liliac replies. "Their hatred vas famous in this *neck* of the woods. I vill tell you more about that on our tour of the castle."

"Come, class!" announces Ms. Frog-bottom. "Mr. Liliac is going to show us upstairs."

We follow Mr. Liliac up a narrow stairway with only ropes to hold on to as we climb. The air is dusty, and other than a few candles on the wall, there's barely any light. The old wooden stairs creak beneath our feet.

"Why would they build a staircase with no banister?" Olivia asks me.

"I have no idea," I admit. "I'm just glad someone put ropes in for tourists like us."

"Why were the steps so narrow?" Olivia asks.

I'm about to check my tablet for an answer, but before I can, Mr. Liliac stops at a room on the next floor. There are thick brown wooden beams on the ceiling, and a real bearskin rug on the floor. Shelves of books line one wall, and there are more paintings of men in velvet robes, as well as an old photograph of Queen Marie. There's also an antique upright piano that looks like it hasn't been played in years.

"Velcome to the library and music room," Mr. Liliac tells us.

"Who played the piano?" Olivia asks him.

"Queen Marie, I believe," Mr. Liliac replies.

He takes Ms. Frogbottom by the hand. "Come, there is a book I would like to show you."

Emma looks down at the rug and frowns. "That poor bear!"

"Who do you think shot it?" Olivia asks. "One of the soldiers? Or a member of Queen Marie's royal family?"

Olivia sure is full of questions today.

I walk over toward one of the bookshelves. That's when I notice something strange about one of the portraits. The eyes seem to be following me around the room as I move.

Of course, that could be an optical illusion. The painter might have drawn the eyes in such a way that it fools you into

thinking they are moving. But it sure does seem like those eyes really are changing direction.

Oddly enough, one eye is green, and the other is blue. It's like Mr. Sange is behind that wall, spying on us.

But what reason would he have to do something like that?

"Check out the piano!" Oliver exclaims. "Hey, Olivia, you want to play 'Heart and Soul' on it with me? I'll let you play the high notes."

Olivia doesn't answer.

Come to think of it, I haven't heard her ask any questions in the past few minutes.

Probably because she's not here anymore.

She's *disappeared*.

7

"WHERE'S OLIVIA?" OLIVER ASKS nervously.

Ms. Frogbottom looks up from the book Mr. Liliac has been showing her. "What do you mean, 'Where's Olivia?'"

"She's not here," Oliver tells her. "She disappeared."

"Don't vorry," Mr. Liliac tells him. "She couldn't go far. No one leaves Bran Castle vithout my knowledge."

Ms. Frogbottom looks at us. "What have I told you all about wandering away from the group?" she demands angrily.

"Why are you mad at us?" Emma asks her. "*We* didn't wander away."

That's actually a very logical question. But Ms. Frogbottom doesn't answer. Instead she calls to our missing classmate. "Olivia! Come out now!"

We stand there, waiting for Olivia to appear. But she doesn't.

"I have to find her!" Oliver heads for the door.

"Oliver, stop!" Ms. Frogbottom orders.

"But she's my sister."

"We'll all go *together* to look for Olivia," Ms. Frogbottom says.

"Come," Mr. Liliac urges. "Ve shall look in the *necks* room."

"Did you hear Mr. Liliac say 'necks' instead of 'next'?" Emma whispers to me.

"It's just his accent," I reply.

"If Olivia's playing hide-and-seek, she's won this round," Aiden says.

"I don't think she's playing anything," Emma tells him. "I think a vampire got her."

Mr. Liliac opens a heavy wooden door that leads to a bedroom. We peer inside. Candlesticks have been placed all over, giving the room an eerie glow.

"I'm not going in there," Tony says. "There are coffins."

He's right. There are two closed dark

wooden coffins in the middle of the room.

"You don't have to worry," Emma tells him. "There won't be any vampires inside those coffins. Vampires only sleep during the day. They emerge after dark." She gives Mr. Liliac a look.

"Olivia, come out now!" Ms. Frogbottom calls in a stern voice.

Olivia doesn't answer.

"Let's try the next room," Ms. Frogbottom says. "She's not in here."

Our teacher and Mr. Liliac head into the hallway through the open door. We kids turn to follow into the hall. But before we can take even a single step—

"BOO!" Suddenly one of the coffin lids flies open, and someone pops out.

"*AAAAAAAAAAH!*" We all let out a shriek. Tony's is the loudest.

"Hahahahahahaha! Gotcha!" Olivia cheers as she climbs out of the coffin. "Boy, you should have seen the looks on your faces. You were really scared."

"That wasn't funny," Tony tells her.

"Sure it was," Olivia says. "You thought

it was funny, didn't you, 'Liver?"

Oliver gives her a dirty look. "I told you never to call me that."

"Ms. Frogbottom's not going to think it was funny," Tony says. "I bet she writes a note home to your parents."

Now it's Olivia's turn to look scared. I don't blame her. Who wants to bring a note home?

Aiden steps into the hallway and calls, "Ms. Frogbottom! We found Olivia!"

Ms. Frogbottom doesn't answer. She's not in the hallway anymore.

Now where did *she* go?

"He's got Ms. Frogbottom!" Emma exclaims.

"Who does?" Aiden asks.

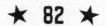

"The vampire," Emma responds. "Mr. Liliac."

"He's *not* a vampire," I insist.

"He is," Emma argues. "I told you he had no reflection in the mirror."

"It was just your imagination," I tell her. "You have a great imagination."

"I do," Emma agrees. "But I didn't imagine him talking about necks and blood."

"It's part of his act, to show off for tourists," I insist.

"And he's avoiding Tony and his garlic," Emma adds.

"*We're all* avoiding Tony and his garlic," I remind her.

Tony stares at the ground and fiddles with the pouch around his neck.

"I'll bet he hypnotized Ms. Frogbottom and dragged her to his lair." Emma's really on a roll now. "He's going to bite her neck and turn her into a vampire."

"That won't happen," I insist. "Vampire legends are fiction."

"Do you have a better explanation?" Aiden asks me. "Because I can't think of any other reason why Ms. Frogbottom would leave us here, all alone, without telling us she was going."

Aiden's got me there. It's not like Ms. Frogbottom to just disappear on us. Unless she's in some sort of trouble.

FROGBOTTOM FACT
★ There are fifty-seven rooms in Bran Castle.

"SHE'S NOT HERE," EMMA SAYS AS WE race into another bedroom. It's the sixth room we've tried, and there's still no sign of our teacher.

I can see why Bram Stoker used this castle as the model for Dracula's castle in his book. It's frighteningly dark and damp inside. The candlelight creates creepy shadows on the walls. And as if all that weren't bad enough, I hear mice scratching from inside the walls, trying to escape.

"Ms. Frogbottom could be hiding," Tony suggests.

I look around the room. It's lit only by a few small candles, but that's enough light for me to see that there's a small bed, a red-and-blue woven rug, a fireplace, and a small carved wooden dresser. There's *no* place to hide.

"Maybe they went back downstairs," Aiden tries.

I shake my head. "We would've heard them. Those wooden stairs are really creaky."

"Maybe Mr. Liliac turned into a bat and flew her to his lair," Emma suggests.

"For the last time, *vampires aren't real*," I insist. "And bats aren't strong enough to carry a teacher."

"Maybe they just disappeared into thin air," Tony suggests. "It could happen."

"Be serious. This is important!" Aiden says. He pushes Tony on the shoulder.

It's just a small push, but Tony tips backward and whacks his shoulder on the wall surrounding the fireplace.

Whoosh! The wall swings open, taking the false fireplace with it.

There's a stairway in there!

"Wow!" Oliver exclaims. "A secret passageway."

"A lot of old castles had them," I say.

"Do you think Mr. Liliac captured Ms.

Frogbottom and took her up those stairs?"
Emma asks me.

"I don't know about *captured*. But I
think it's possible they could be up there."

"Let's go get her," Aiden tells me.

"Oh no," Tony argues. "You remember the last time we went through a tiny

doorway like that? We got locked in a tomb of doom."

"But she's our teacher," Aiden insists. "We have to find her."

"Would you rather stay in Transylvania forever?" Olivia asks Tony. "Ms. Frogbottom had her backpack with her when she disappeared. And you know what's in that pack. . . ."

"The Magic Map," Tony says.

FROGBOTTOM FACTS

★ The actual secret passageway in Bran Castle was originally built as an escape tunnel for soldiers in case of an attack. The passage ran from the first floor to the watchtower of the castle.

★ The passageway was such a secret that it was forgotten for hundreds of years. It was found in the 1920s when Queen Marie was renovating the castle.

Olivia nods. "Our ticket home."

Tony sighs. "Fine. I'll go. But I don't like it."

I don't like it either. But we have no choice. I pull out my tablet and click on the flashlight app so we're able to see in the darkness. We start walking up the stairs. They're made of stone, which explains why they didn't creak when Ms. Frogbottom took them.

If Ms. Frogbottom took these stairs. We still don't know that for sure.

The stone walls on either side are so close together, they feel as though they're closing in on us. I figure the people who originally climbed these stairs had to have gone single file. And hurried. No one would want to be in this hidden stairwell for very long. I sure don't.

Finally we reach the top. We gather together tightly on the landing, and peer in through an open door.

Inside is a tiny room, lit only by candles and the moonlight streaming in through a single, small window. There's an open coffin on the floor.

Mr. Liliac is standing in the middle of the room, holding a bell. Ms. Frogbottom is standing beside him. She doesn't look scared at all. In fact, she's smiling calmly. Almost *too* calmly. It's like she's in a trance.

"Vell, now ve shall see if you vill follow my commands," Mr. Liliac says to Ms.

Frogbottom. He rings a bell. And the next thing we know . . .

"Cluck. Cluck."

Our teacher is clucking like a chicken. She has her hands under her armpits, and she's flapping her bent arms like wings. She's kicking her feet behind her and moving her head back and forth like she's a bird pecking at seeds.

"I know that dance. It's called the funky chicken," Emma whispers. "My uncle Nate

FROGBOTTOM FACTS

★ A person who is hypnotized is put into a trance. This allows the hypnotist to make suggestions that can change that person's behavior.
★ Some people are more easily hypnotized than others.

did it at my cousin Max's bar mitzvah. But why is Ms. Frogbottom doing it now?"

"I think he hypnotized her," I answer. "Every time she hears that bell, she'll do the dance."

"Why would he want her to do that?" Emma asks me.

"It could be a test," I say quietly. "To see if she can be hypnotized. Not everybody can be put under a hypnotic spell."

"Ms. Frogbottom can," Emma points out. "Look at her."

"Cluck. Cluck."

Emma's right. Mr. Liliac has hypnotized our teacher—the same way vampires in books and movies hypnotize their victims.

Just the thought of Ms. Frogbottom as a victim makes me sad. And afraid.

"Ms. Frogbottom's under Mr. Liliac's control now," Emma whispers. "It's going to make it easier for him to bite her neck."

I start to argue with Emma about vampires, but I stop. Because I actually think she may be right.

At some point you have to accept what the evidence tells you. And right now the evidence is telling me that vampires are real, and Mr. Liliac is one of them.

Maybe I could find excuses for how he is always talking about blood and necks and why he's staying far away from Tony. But he's hypnotizing Ms. Frogbottom. It's not like he's doing *that* to show off for an audience. It's just the two of them in there. And if what Emma said about him not having a reflection is actually true, then it all adds up to one thing.

Our teacher is in trouble. Because before the sun rises, that vampire is likely to get hungry. He's probably going to want to go for a bite . . .

Of Ms. Frogbottom's neck!

9

"WE HAVE TO SAVE OUR TEACHER!" EMMA says.

We're back in the entranceway of Bran Castle. Hopefully that's far enough away from Mr. Liliac that he can't overhear us talking about him—even with powerful bat hearing.

"How? He's a vampire," Tony asks Emma. "We're just kids. That's not a fair fight."

"Vampires do have the superpowers of the undead," Emma agrees.

"But there are ways to defeat a vampire, right?" Olivia asks.

Emma thinks for a minute. "To get rid of him once and for all we would have to put a stake through his heart."

"Maybe we should go back to the café and get a steak then," Aiden suggests. "Do we have to cook it first?"

I shake my head. "Not the kind of steak that's meat," I tell him. "The kind of stake that's a knife."

My friends stare at Emma and me.

"Are you crazy?" Tony asks me. "We can't do that."

"If you set a vampire on fire," Emma continues, "that would get rid of him."

"We can do *that*, either," Tony insists.

He's right, of course. "There has to be something less gruesome," I say.

"I saw one movie where the vampire ate garlic and then began to disintegrate," Emma tries.

That's it!

"We need to go back to the café," I tell my classmates. "I need ingredients."

"This is no time to cook," Oliver tells me.

"I'm only *cooking up* a plan," I assure him.

"We can't go outside," Tony insists. "It's dark and scary."

"We have to do *something*," Emma tells him. "Sofia's the only one of us with an idea. Unless *you* have a plan?"

Tony scrunches his lips. He scratches

his hair. And tilts his head. "I got nothing," he admits.

"That settles it!" I fling open the heavy wooden door and run out into the Transylvanian night. "Come on."

"We ran down that mountain for *ketchup*?" Olivia asks breathlessly as we arrive at the outdoor café.

The restaurant is closed now. The square is empty. It's late. Most people have gone home. Being at an empty, dark outdoor café in the middle of Transylvania, with Bran Castle looking down at us, is really spooky. But I can't think about that now. There's no time to be scared.

"Ms. Frogbottom never put this bottle

back into her pack," I tell Olivia. "I'm just glad the waiter left it on the table."

"I'm sweating from my hair to my socks," Aiden complains. "This better be good, Sofia."

"It will be good," Emma assures him.

She doesn't add that it will be good because I'm the class brain. Emma isn't saying anything mean to me now. Maybe because she was the first one to realize that Mr. Liliac really was a vampire, so she feels pretty smart too.

"Why do we need ketchup?" Oliver asks.

"I'm going to rub it on my neck," I explain. "It'll look like blood. I'm hoping that when Mr. Liliac sees it, he's going to want to come for that blood. And while he's focused on me, you guys can rescue Ms. Frogbottom."

"But if he bites your neck, he'll turn you into a vampire," Tony points out.

"He's not going to get close to me," I reply.

"Why not?" Oliver asks me.

"I'm going to mix garlic with the ketchup.  When he smells that, he'll want to make a quick escape."

"By turning into a bat," Emma adds. "He'll just fly off and leave us alone."

"That's the plan," I say.

"It won't work," Olivia insists.

"Why not?" I ask her.

"They don't cook with garlic here, remember?" she replies.

Of course I remember. I remember everything. But I don't say that. Instead I say, "There's another place I can get it. Tony, give me your necklace."

"No way," Tony says. "Garlic's the only reason I'm not getting mosquito bites."

He looks at us.

We look back at him.

Finally he unties the leather cord and hands me the pouch.

I take out the clove of garlic and peel it open. Then . . . BAM. I use my fist to smash the garlic into little pieces. I pour some ketchup onto one of the paper napkins on the table and mix it with the smashed garlic.

Boy, does that stink.

As I rub the ketchup-garlic mush onto my neck, I have the strangest feeling someone is watching us.

I hear a rustling in the nearby trees. It's pretty dark, so I can't say *for sure* that I see anyone sitting in the branches, but I could swear there are two eyes staring at us: one blue and one green.

"Do you guys see someone in that tree?" I ask.

Everyone looks up. But whoever was there has disappeared.

Maybe it was my imagination. Or not.

"Let's get out of here," I say. "Mr. Liliac will be happy making Ms. Frogbottom
dance the funky chicken for only so long.
He's going to get hungry for blood soon."

ARRROOOOOOO! As we pass a thicket
of pine trees, we hear howling . . . again.

A shiver runs up my spine. I was wrong
about vampires not being real. I might have
been wrong about capcauns, too. Maybe
there really *are* four-eyed dog-ogres roam-
ing Transylvania looking for kids to eat.

ARRROOOOOOO!

A really horrible stink fills the air.

I stare into the trees. Four big, dark
eyes stare back at me.

"CAPCAUN! RUN!" Aiden shouts.

"We can't outrun a capcaun," I argue. "He's part dog. You know how fast dogs can run."

"We're doomed!" Tony cries.

"So is Ms. Frogbottom," Emma adds sadly.

"Not necessarily," I insist. "We can't outrun him, but maybe we can out*smart* him."

Tony shakes his head. "Capcauns are smart. Mr. Sange said they trick kids into becoming their dinner."

"I bet capcauns aren't smarter than Sofia." Emma smiles at me. "What's your plan?"

I don't actually have one. But I'd better think of something quickly. I can hear that capcaun breathing hungrily. And I'm pretty sure *we're* what he's hungry for!

"We need your sock, Aiden," I say finally.

"Why?" he asks me. "It's all sweaty."

"Exactly," I reply. "I need the smelliest, sweatiest sock possible."

Aiden shrugs. "Okay. You asked for it."

He peels off his stinky sock and goes to hand it to me. But there's no way I am touching that thing. Instead I say, "Stick a rock inside it. Then roll it up into a ball and pitch it into the woods and down the mountain—as hard as you can."

"Why stick a rock in it?" Aiden asks me.

"It will go farther with a little extra weight."

"Makes sense," Aiden agrees. He pauses for a second and then asks me, "Why exactly am I throwing my sock, anyway?"

AROOOOOOO!

Because of that.

"Do it!" I insist. To be honest, I'm not sure this plan will work. But it's the only plan we've got right now.

So Aiden puts a rock into his sock and throws it. Hard. It flies into the woods and out of sight. That was some throw. We're lucky Aiden is such a good athlete.

Now we have to hope that the cap-caun will take the bait. My classmates are counting on this plan to work. Which is a lot of pressure on me. I may be really smart, but I'm still just a kid.

A kid who really doesn't want to be a capcaun's late-night snack.

The capcaun's four eyes, which have been focused on us through the trees, turn away.

Sniff. Sniff. Sniff. I hear the capcaun sniffing at the air. Then I hear leaves and twigs crackling in the woods as he runs after Aiden's stinky sock.

Phew! The capcaun has picked up Aiden's scent on the sock, like a dog would. He's chasing the scent of what he thinks is a kid.

But soon he'll realize that it's no kid—

FROGBOTTOM FACT

★ Transylvania got its name partly from the Latin word "silva," which means "forest." "Transylvania" literally means "the land beyond the forests."

just a smelly, sweaty gym sock. Which will make him madder than ever.

"*Now* we run!" I say.

"Hey! Wait for me!" Aiden cries out as he jams his foot back into his shoe and hurries to catch up.

10

LUB-DUB. LUB-DUB.

My heart is pounding. Not because we ran up a mountain and climbed hundreds of stairs to reach the door to Bran Castle.

My heart's pounding because I'm really nervous. I can't believe the vampire is real. But he is. And this is *really* happening.

We're standing silently at the top of the hidden staircase, right outside Mr. Liliac's vampire lair. My classmates are watching

as I prepare to enter the room and set my plan in action.

I put a lot of thought into this plot. I considered every last detail. But that doesn't guarantee it's going to work. In every experiment—and this is really only an experiment because I've never tried it before—there's always a chance something could go wrong. Which would be really dangerous. Especially for me.

I can't worry about that now. Mr. Liliac is getting closer and closer to Ms. Frogbottom. He's moving in slow motion, like a vampire in an old black-and-white movie.

I can't see Mr. Liliac's face because he's turned away from us. But I can imagine his mouth wide open and his fangs poised to take a bite of my teacher's neck. The thought of it is frightening.

You would think Ms. Frogbottom would be scared to death. But she doesn't seem frightened at all. She's sitting there, looking up at him with this strange, goofy expression on her face. She's not trying to run or fight back. I think Mr. Liliac's got her so hypnotized that she can't.

Thump-bump. Thump-bump.

I hear footsteps coming up the stairs behind me. My classmates and I are all here. So who . . . ?

"Master! Be careful. They are plotting against you!"

It's Mr. Sange. He *has* been spying on us. Just like I thought. He *had* to have been. How else would he have known about our plan?

Suddenly it all makes sense. Mr. Sange isn't only a gardener. He's Mr. Liliac's faithful servant. He brings the vampire fresh victims and keeps away his enemies.

Now I get it: Mr. Sange invited us to the castle so that Ms. Frogbottom could be Mr. Liliac's next victim. And Mr. Sange

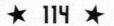

spied on us so he could report on our every move and keep us from getting in the way. Mr. Sange wasn't going to let a bunch of kids stop Mr. Liliac from turning Ms. Frogbottom into a vampire.

I wouldn't be surprised if Mr. Sange somehow let the capcaun know where we were, in order to keep us out of Mr. Liliac's way while he took a bite of Ms. Frogbottom.

Mr. Liliac turns toward us. I can see the anger in his face. Which is terrible. I can't think of a single good thing that can happen when a vampire is mad at you.

Mr. Liliac's eyes fall to my neck. His mouth breaks into a wide grin. His bright, white, pointy fangs glow in the dim light.

Lub-dub. Lub-dub. My heart pounds harder. Those fangs look sharp.

Mr. Liliac takes a few steps toward me. I wait for the garlic scent to ward him off. But it doesn't. That vampire keeps walking toward me.

Closer.

And closer.

And closer still. I can feel his hot breath on me, which means . . .

My plan's not working. Something has gone *very* wrong.

Mr. Liliac is going to bite my neck. He's going to turn me into a vampire. I will become one of the undead.

My mind starts racing. What will it feel like to be a vampire? Will my brain work the same way? Vampires live forever. Does that mean I will remember every single thing I read and hear from now through all eternity? That would be a lot of information. Will I—

"Sofia! Run!" Emma cries.

She's right. I *should* run. I should scream. I should do something.

But I can't. I am literally frozen with fear. I can't seem to move a muscle.

Mr. Liliac leans in toward me. And . . .

"AAAAAAH!" Mr. Liliac lets out a scream. He sniffs at the air around me. And backs away. He must smell the garlic.

The vampire leaps up into the air.

But he doesn't come down.

Instead he shrinks to the size of a fist.

Two black-brown wings sprout from his back. The vampire is shape-shifting into a bat. Right before our very eyes.

The Mr. Liliac–bat flies out through the small open window and disappears into the dark Romanian night.

"Master! Wait for me!" Mr. Sange cries as he races toward the window. He climbs out onto the balcony. "Do not leave me!"

Now we are alone in the vampire's den. Just the six of us kids.

And our teacher, who is staring into space with a goofy look on her face.

I take a deep breath and let it out slowly. That was close. Really close. Way *too* close.

"You did it!"

"Sofia, you're amazing!"

"You are one brave brainiac!"

My classmates are surrounding me and cheering. They're congratulating me on being smart, instead of making fun of me for it. That feels really good.

It also feels really good not to be a vampire. Things got pretty close there for a second.

"Olivia!" Ms. Frogbottom leaps to her feet. "We've been looking all over for you."

"We found her a while—" Aiden begins.

I nudge his side to keep him quiet. Ms. Frogbottom has been under a hypnotic spell. She probably doesn't realize that any time has gone by. Telling her we found Olivia a while ago would only confuse her.

Ms. Frogbottom looks at me. "Sofia, you need to stop scratching your mosquito bites. You've made the one on your neck bleed."

My fake blood really must look very real. It fooled a vampire *and* a teacher.

"Okay, so now that we're all together, why don't we continue our tour of Bran Castle?" Ms. Frogbottom glances around the room. "I wonder where Mr. Liliac has gotten to."

"I think I heard him say something about having to *take off*," Emma replies.

"He just *flew* out of here," Olivia jokes.

"Oh." Ms. Frogbottom sounds disappointed. "Well, never mind. I'm sure we can still learn a lot touring the castle without him."

"No!" Tony exclaims. "I've seen enough of this place."

"But we haven't visited the kitchen yet," Ms. Frogbottom tells him. "Or the courtyard. Or . . ." Our teacher gazes around the room. A confused look comes over her face. "I must be getting tired. I barely remember coming up here. I'm not sure what this room was used for hundreds of years ago, but I'm sure Mr. Liliac knows."

"I'm sure he does too," Emma whispers to me. "Vampires live forever. He was probably *here* hundreds of years ago."

I don't need Mr. Liliac to tell me the purpose of this room. We all know it's a vampire lair, where Mr. Liliac spends his nights feeding on the blood of innocent victims, and his days sleeping in a coffin bed. Which is why we really need to get out of here. That vampire needs to be back in his coffin before the sun comes up. We have to be gone before he returns.

I let out a huge fake yawn. Actually, it's not so fake. This has been a long night. "Would it be okay if we went back to camp now?" I ask Ms. Frogbottom. "I want to be alert for tomorrow's water experiments."

Emma lets out a big yawn too. "I'm ready for sleep," she agrees. "Lala Radala always says, 'Get eight hours' rest to look your best.'"

The yawning is contagious. Now all my classmates have their mouths open.

"I suppose we should go back," Ms. Frogbottom agrees as she pulls the Magic Map from her backpack. "Tomorrow is another day."

Ms. Frogbottom places her finger on the map. Suddenly a white light flashes all around us. My body feels weightless, and I think my feet have just left the ground.

It's like I'm flying in space. And then . . .

11

"MAY I HAVE ANOTHER TEST TUBE?" I ASK

Ms. Frogbottom. We are collecting water

samples from the creek at science camp this

morning, and there's a particularly brown

batch near the shore I'd like to test.

"Of course, Sofia," Ms. Frogbottom says.

She reaches into her backpack and pulls

out a glass tube.

ROAROOO!

Suddenly we hear an animal howling in

the woods. My classmates and I all stop in our tracks and listen.

ROAROOO!

"It can't be," Olivia says.

"Of course not," Oliver agrees.

"Capcauns are only in Romania, right?" Tony adds.

I am about to tell Tony he's right, and then a really bad smell fills the air. Now I'm not too sure.

There's a rustling in the nearby trees. Something is moving toward us. That smell is getting stronger and stronger.

ROAROOO...

"Oomf!" Tony lets out a groan as he's knocked to the ground by a fast-running puppy.

A *very* smelly puppy.

"Get off me," Tony says as the stinky pup licks his face and jumps all over him. "You smell."

"Now you know how we felt about your garlic," Olivia tells him.

"Why does that puppy smell so bad?" Emma wonders.

"The poor thing's been sprayed by a skunk," Ms. Frogbottom tells us.

"Now *I* smell skunky," Tony groans.

Just then a tall, thin man comes running our way.

"Who's that?" Oliver wonders.

"I don't know," Ms. Frogbottom replies.

"He's not a vampire," Emma says. "He wouldn't be out in broad daylight if he were."

"Frisky! There you are," the man calls out.

The puppy leaps off Tony. His tail wags wildly as he runs toward his owner.

"I'm so glad these kids found you," the man tells Frisky. He sniffs at the air. "I see you've met up with a skunk."

"And now the skunk stink is all over *me*," Tony tells him.

"I'm sorry," the man replies. "Frisky always seems to be getting into trouble with the skunks at this science campground. My family and I live just down the road. We've had to give Frisky skunk-smell treatments more times than I can count."

"There are *treatments*?" Tony repeats the word hopefully.

"Of course," the man replies. "All you have to do is take a bath in a lot of tomato juice."

"*Blood-red* tomato juice," Emma says. She lets out a little giggle.

"Is there any other kind?" Frisky's owner asks curiously.

Now we kids are all laughing.

Ms. Frogbottom looks at us. "What's so funny?" she asks.

"Nothing," I answer. There's no way we can explain this to Ms. Frogbottom.

"Here you go, Tony." Ms. Frogbottom reaches into her backpack and pulls out three huge cans of tomato juice. "You've got to get rid of that smell. The sooner the better."

"You smell like fresh, chopped tomatoes," Emma tells Tony a while later after he's washed and shampooed himself with tomato juice. "It's definitely better than smelling like a skunk."

"Or garlic," Oliver adds. "That stuff

was nasty. Not as nasty as skunk, but pretty bad."

I know for a fact that the tomato juice didn't wash away the skunk's odor. It's masking the terrible smell. Under all that tomato, Tony still smells like a skunk. But I don't say anything. I'm trying really hard not to share *every* fact that's stored in my memory. There's a difference between being smart and being a know-it-all.

Besides, Tony will find that out all on his own, when the tomato smell wears off.

"The smell of tomatoes is making me hungry," Aiden says. "Is it lunchtime yet?"

Ms. Frogbottom glances at her watch. "We should be hearing the dining hall bell any minute now," she tells him.

RRRRIIIIINNNNGGG.

Sure enough, the loud bell outside the dining hall rings throughout the campground. It's time for lunch.

Ms. Frogbottom should be leading us up the hill to the dining hall. But instead of walking, our teacher stops in her tracks and begins to . . .

"Cluck! Cluck!"

Ms. Frogbottom is flapping her arms up and down. She's kicking her feet backward. And moving her head back and forth.

The other class groups at the campground stop and circle around her. Some of the kids look confused. Others seem amazed. A lot of them are laughing.

"How long does this hypnosis thing last?" Emma asks me.

"I don't know," I answer honestly. "But as soon as I'm someplace where I can get service on my tablet, I'm going to look up how to *unhypnotize* someone. Because this is just embarrassing."

"Cluck! Cluck!" Ms. Frogbottom shouts again. "Clu-u-u-ck!"

"So, did you have a good time at science camp?" my father asks me later that

afternoon when we meet up with our parents back at the Left Turn Alleyway Elementary parking lot.

"Definitely," I tell him. "You know how much I love field trips." I let out a big yawn.

"No one gets a whole lot of sleep on overnights," my father says. "I remember when my friends and I would go on camping trips. We'd be up all night telling scary stories, and then we'd wind up napping the next day. It was like we became vampires for a few days." He gives me a big smile.

Vampires?

I look over nervously at his mouth. *Phew.* No fangs there. I guess it was just a figure of speech.

Well, that's a relief.

WORDS YOU HEAR ON A FIELD TRIP TO ROMANIA

ancestor: A relative who lived several generations before someone

capcaun: A four-eyed ogre with a dog's head; according to Romanian folklore, capcauns kidnap children and princesses

citadel: A fortress built on high ground, meant to protect a city

cobblestone: A small, round stone used to cover the surface of a road

drawbridge: A bridge, often above a castle moat, that is hinged at one end so that it